GW00865048

Tom has a pet hamster in his room. The hamster is called Charlie.

1

Charlie has a hamster ball. He whizzes round Tom's bedroom in his ball.

Crash! Oh no! The ball hits a leg of the bed. It comes open and it falls apart.

Charlie looks out of the broken ball. Tigga and Fluff are coming towards him.

Charlie runs under the bed. The cats squeeze under the bed after him. Clatter! Bang!

Trains and cars fly out from under the bed as the cats try to find Charlie.

Tigga and Fluff come out from under the bed. They have not found Charlie the hamster.

Tigga and Fluff give up. They go away. Where is Charlie? He is hiding in a truck.